This Princess Can...

Author: Jane E. Sparrow   Illustrator: Diandra Hwan

MONCREIFFE
— PRESS

Illustrator Diandra Hwan
Editor Jennifer Waddle

Paperback ISBN 978-1-8384798-0-0

Published by Moncreiffe Press
press@moncreiffe.org.uk

For my parents, Michael and Diana

This princess can...

dance a pirouette

and quickly climb a tree,

scale a lofty mountain

or sail on silver seas.

She can brave an angry dragon

and aid a knight to flee,

help them make good friends again

and invite them round for tea.

This princess can...  read books

that make her imagination soar,

discover exciting new things

that have never been found before.

She can laze beside a trickling stream

or trek through forests deep,

make the most of what each new day brings

and make promises to keep.

This princess can...

dig for buried treasure

and explore uncharted lands,

boldly reach towards her dreams

...even for things unplanned.

She can make friends with nobles

and people everywhere,

for she knows that life's adventures are best enjoyed

with friends who truly care.

The End

About the Author

Jane E. Sparrow is a writer living in Scotland, and author of the new children's book 'This Princess Can...'. Jane has a master's degree in English & Scottish Literature from The University of Edinburgh, and this is her first work of fiction.

To sign up to receive email updates about new and upcoming releases, visit: *press.moncreiffe.org.uk*

Printed in Great Britain
by Amazon